# Mariella Mystery

## Investigates

## A kitty CALAMITY

# Never miss a clue!

Join our **Mariella Mystery Investigates Club** for the latest news on your favorite sleuth-y detective, plus:

- A club certificate and membership card
- **Mariella Mystery** games, activities, puzzles, and coloring pages
- Excerpts from the books and news about forthcoming titles
- Contests for **FREE** stuff

You can become the next Young Super Sleuth—just like Mariella!

Visit **barronsbooks.com/mariella/** today and join in the fun!

Open to U.S. residents only.

## Certificate

This is to certify that

_____

is an official member in good standing of

## Mariella Mystery
### Investigates Club

and entitled to all rights & privileges

granted this _____ day of _____

 **Look out for more books about Mariella Mystery**

The Spaghetti Yeti
The Kitty Calamity
The Ghostly Guinea Pig
A Cupcake Conundrum
The Huge Hair Scare
The Curse of the Pampered Poodle

(#296) R12/14

# Mariella Mystery Investigates

## A kitty CALAMITY

by Kate Pankhurst

BARRON'S

First edition for the United States published in 2015
by Barron's Educational Series, Inc.

First published in Great Britain in 2014 by Orion Children's Books,
a division of the Orion Publishing Group Ltd., Orion House,
5 Upper St. Martin's Lane, London WC2H 9EA, Great Britain

*All inquiries should be addressed to:*
Barron's Educational Series, Inc.
250 Wireless Boulevard, Hauppauge, New York 11788
**www.barronseduc.com**

ISBN: 978-1-4380-0704-5

Library of Congress Control No. 2014935200

Manufactured by M19A19R, Louiseville (Quebec), Canada

Date of Manufacture: April 2015

Printed in Canada

9 8 7 6 5 4 3 2 1

For Lucy, James, and Sue

# THIS YOUNG SUPER SLEUTH JOURNAL BELONGS TO ...

Mariella Mystery . . . that's me! Totally amazing (not quite world famous yet) detective, aged nine and three quarters.

I'd like to spend less time writing about the stupid stuff my little brother Arthur does in this, my top-secret detective's journal. But I don't think that will happen any time soon, because he is incapable of being anything other than completely annoying.

Arthur. Small and talks in a high-pitched squeak.

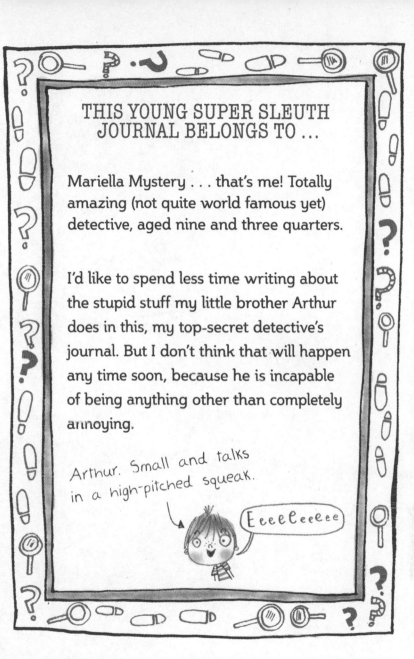

Eeeeeeeeee

# Sunday
# April 19th

mystery HQ

## 7:00 PM
## MYSTERY GIRLS HQ, TREE HOUSE IN MY BACKYARD

It's important to take every mystery situation seriously. That's why I totally can't be blamed for what just happened.

## CASE REVIEW

## THE NOWHERE-TO-BE-SEEN KITTY-NEXT-DOOR

## Henry

Henry

Currently Missing Cat of our distraught next-door neighbor, Josie Jones. Hasn't come home for three days. We've searched everywhere for him. Last seen wearing a glittery red collar.

Josie (neighbor) ⟶

## MYSTERY GIRL INVESTIGATORS:

## Violet Maple

Allergic to everything—including cats—but that doesn't stop her from being an amazing detective.

Violet

## Poppy Holmes

We thought she might be related to Sherlock Holmes (world-famous detective) because she is so good at finding clues, but then found out Sherlock Holmes is a made-up person in a book. Oh well. Poppy is still a talented Mystery Girl and synchronized swimmer.

POPPY in a
sherlock Holmes hat

Sherlock Holmes

Me and Watson 🐾

# Mariella Mystery

I'm not sure Henry's disappearance is going to make us famous detectives, because when cats go missing it's usually because they are stuck up trees or have found a new owner who feeds them tastier food. There aren't any more complicated mysteries happening at the moment, though, so we've agreed to take on the case. (Also I'd be totally upset if Watson, trusty sidekick and pet cat, disappeared.)

## CASE REVIEW MEETING GETS MYSTERIOUS

**5:50 PM**: In HQ, Poppy has totally distracted me and Violet by using Watson as a model for our new set of detective fake mustaches.

cute

mustaches →

12

**5:55 PM:** A piercing scream from outside HQ makes us all jump. Watson hides under the Mystery Desk.

spooked

**5:56 PM:** The screamer is quickly identified. Arthur is standing under the tree house shouting hysterically "stuck in tree" and "fluffy."

screamer

**5:58 PM:** Looking up through the leaves above HQ, there is a flash of orange fur. Henry! I can't believe he has been here all along. I launch a tree-scaling rescue attempt.

**6:02 PM:** Gripping the tree with one hand, I reach toward Henry's bottom, which is poking through the leaves.

FURRY BOTTOM!

**6:03 PM:** I realize the fluffy orange thing is most definitely NOT Henry. I have just risked everything to rescue... Arthur's fluffy kitten slipper.

FLUFFY kitten SLIPPER!

13

**6:04 PM:** Josie from next door comes out of her house just as I'm flinging the slipper at Arthur's head. She also mistakes the slipper for Henry and shrieks. (Honestly, as if I'd fling the real Henry at Arthur's head.) Watson, distressed by all the noise, bolts from HQ, still wearing the fake mustache.

**6:05 PM:** Mom comes outside. She sees me in the tree and shouts at me to get down. I can't. I am stuck.

**6:45 PM:** Dad arrives home from work and I, elite Mystery Girl, have to be rescued from the tree while everyone watches. It's completely embarrassing and it's all Arthur's fault. And we still have no idea where Henry is.

mystery bed

## 8:00 PM
## MY BEDROOM, MAD AT ARTHUR

I just hope Watson is still wearing that
mustache when he comes back. It's the best in
our collection. It's Arthur's fault that Watson ran
away wearing it, so he WILL be replacing
it with his allowance if it's lost.

LOST

At least there's some other cool stuff to
look forward to. It's Puddleford Festival
time again! Poppy says we have to
synchronize our alarm clocks on
Saturday because you need to
arrive early if you don't want
to wait on line for
the totally spooky
ghost train or the
helter-skelter rides.

Helter-Skelter

viole

Poppy

GHOST TRAIN

me

Oh, and I've discovered that this year's festival theme, Pioneers of Puddleford, has actually nothing to do with pies. Pioneers of Puddleford are actually people who have achieved great things and made Puddleford a cool place to live.

**LADY WINKLETON:** Set up Puddleford Museum one hundred years ago. We totally solved a mystery about her stuffed poodle.

**LIZBETH FELANGE:** Founded Kitty Yum Luxury Cat Products, here in Puddleford. Kitty Yum is now a worldwide success and this year's festival sponsor.

**MOM (AKA MRS. MYSTERY):** Runs online knitting shop called Knitted Fancies (You Name It, We'll Knit It). The first person ever to knit a miniature model of Puddleford. She's running a Knit Your Own Miniature Puddleford demonstration at the festival.

miniature PUDDLEFORD

me → inventing stuff

I couldn't believe it when our totally awesome teacher, Miss Crumble, announced that we'd all be entering a new Best in Show Young Inventors competition at the festival. Everyone in our school is going to get a chance to be a Pioneer of Puddleford too! We are even going to have another Pioneer of Puddleford helping us all week in school—a real-life inventor!

**HORATIO TWEED:** We met Horatio briefly once while doing a surveillance sweep of Puddleford. (The Young Super Sleuth's Handbook recommends this if things are quiet.) He looks like a mad scientist but his house on Blossom Lane is totally normal. I bet he has to make it seem that way, so nobody suspects he's making amazing top-secret inventions inside.

Horatio Tweed ↴

Detectives in films always have a genius inventor friend with a mysterious nickname, like Z or Nuts, who makes gadgets for them—like lunchboxes that turn into rocket packs.* We could be sitting in the school cafeteria, and if a call came in about an urgent mystery situation—WHOOSH!— we'd fire up the lunchbox and jet off to investigate before the teachers could say anything.

Maybe Horatio will agree to be our cool inventor friend who will do stuff like that for us? I hope so!

WOW!

LUNCH

looks normal

*THE LUNCH LAUNCHER was one of the brilliant ideas that Poppy, Violet, and I came up with as part of our homework. Miss Crumble said we can work together. Yay!

Deduction 'o' matic

# GADGETS AND MYSTERY SOLVING

Sometimes fake mustaches and dark sunglasses are not enough. Gadgets will make you the most envied detective in town but it's essential to pick the right device for the type of mystery situation you are in.

## Types of Gadgets:

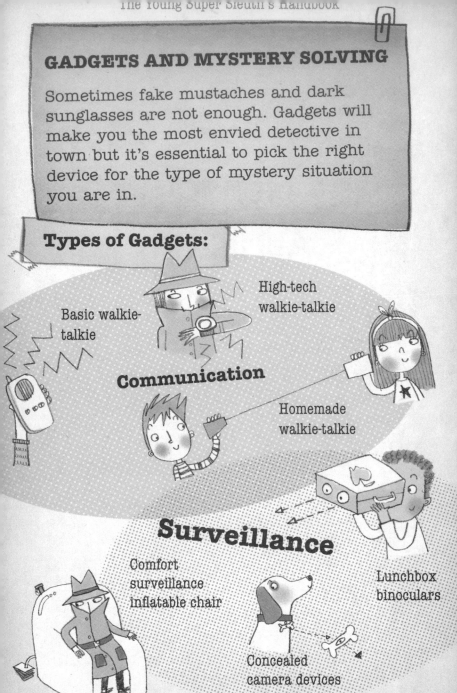

High-tech walkie-talkie

Basic walkie-talkie

**Communication**

Homemade walkie-talkie

# Surveillance

Comfort surveillance inflatable chair

Lunchbox binoculars

Concealed camera devices

## Suspect Capturing

Net launchers

Robotic capturing devices

Battery powered skates (for chase situations)

## Fancy gadgets

X-ray glasses

Cough-it-up confession sweets

I dunnit!

Rocket-powered underpants

# WARNING

Don't let Fancy Gadget Fever cloud your mystery senses. We hear many stories of detective teams falling apart after heated arguments over whose turn it is to use the new gadget or about whose gadget is the best.

## 10:10 AM
## SCHOOL HALL, WHOLE SCHOOL ASSEMBLY

Horatio isn't here yet but one of his inventions is set up at the front of the hall. It's got flashing buttons, knobs, and spinning things on it. Violet said I was being over the top when I thought it might be a teleportation device. You never know.

There's also a table lined with test tubes and bottles of chemicals. We are going to get a sneak preview of the live experiment Horatio will be demonstrating at the Puddleford Festival. Cool!

mad scientist's Lab!

Veronica

It's a little annoying that Veronica Spent from our class has managed to get a really good spot right at the front of the room where all the little kids like Arthur sit. How did she persuade Miss Crumble to let her do that?

(I'm still angry with Arthur—I couldn't find Watson anywhere this morning—he must be totally traumatized after the fuss yesterday.)

Josie's cat Henry has still not come home. Last night I kept watch for him from my bedroom window. There was no sign, so I sketched some ideas for inventions instead. I've just shown Poppy and Violet—they think we should totally ask Horatio how to build a control panel in HQ. It will be voice-activated by a Mystery Girl, so if Arthur tries to go near it, an alarm will sound and shutters will come down, locking Arthur inside until I can deal with him!

Beep

Beep

mystery control center

## 11:15 AM
## PUDDLEFORD ELEMENTARY,
## GIRLS' BATHROOMS

We've been stuck in the bathrooms for half an hour now, all because Poppy volunteered to take part in Horatio's experiment. This turned out to be a BAD IDEA.

"Every day I try to think up new inventions—like the Never-Ending Pencil and my Whiff-o-Matic Smelly Sock Detector," Horatio said, after Miss Crumble had introduced him.

He pressed the buttons on his machine and it began to whirr, chug, and rattle. Everyone went *oooooooohhh!*

This was the part where Horatio would tell us it was an invisibility machine or a clue detector or something.

"Behold the Fresh Fingers Garbage!" Horatio said. "My vision of the future is one where nobody has to touch a garbage and risk coming into contact with moldy teabags again!"

A garbage emptier? Of all the things an inventor could invent, Horatio picked a garbage emptier? It was totally not my idea of exciting, but Miss Crumble looked delighted as the machine emptied the garbage Horatio had brought from the faculty room. At least, she did until it jammed and shredded paper and apple cores flew out and hit Arthur, his annoying friend Pippa, and a few other kids from his class in the front row.

"Just a few teething problems! All part of the inventing process!" Horatio said.

I hoped Horatio had some other cool stuff to show us.

mush

Next, he stepped forward and proudly held up a glass jar with some mush in it.

"Now for what you've all been waiting for—a sneak preview of the invention I will be launching at the Puddleford Festival," he said. "Soon nobody will need fillings at the dentist EVER again! This Pooka-Pooka leaf extract was sent to me by Chief Numpopo, leader of the Rara tribe, who lives deep in the Amazonian rain forest. They are known for their sparkling teeth. This is the ingredient that makes Mega Watt Grin Paste the world's most effective toothpaste!"

Everyone oooohed again.

chief numpopo

Horatio showed us how he brewed the toothpaste by heating test tubes until hot gloop traveled through pipes and white and blue stripy toothpaste squeezed into a beaker at the other end. (It seemed like a lot of effort just for toothpaste.)

When Horatio asked for a volunteer to come to the front and test the toothpaste, Poppy's hand was first to go up. She loves doing stuff like this.

"Are you ready, Poppy, to experience the hurricane foaming action? A minty explosion of freshness and a sparkling smile?" Horatio said, passing Poppy a toothbrush.

"Bring it on!" Poppy said, grinning.

But as soon as Poppy started brushing, her grin changed to an expression of disgust and confusion.

27

Poppy's cheeks bulged,
then tons of white foam
burst out of her mouth onto
the floor. The whole hall erupted
into hysterical laughter.

Foam kept spraying out of Poppy's mouth. Horatio
kept apologizing. Miss Crumble tried to keep
everyone from laughing, but it was useless. Arthur
and Pippa and the other kids in the front row were
squealing because foam had splattered on them.

Veronica Spent stood up and ran out of the hall. I
think she was crying! I was really surprised. Getting
so upset about having some toothpaste on her
seemed like a total overreaction, especially since
Poppy was the one with a real problem.

Hmmm. Horatio isn't exactly the science genius
I'd been hoping for.

experimental toothpaste

## 12:30 PM
## PUDDLEFORD ELEMENTARY, CAFETERIA

The Young Super Sleuth's Handbook says that when people act out of character, it can be a sign that they are worried and need the help of a detective. So, I should have guessed there was something weird going on—and I'm not talking about experimental toothpaste.

After Poppy's mouth stopped foaming, we headed back to class. I wondered whether Horatio would have been told not to come back to school ever again. (Turns out he hasn't, but Miss Twist, our head teacher, has banned him from doing any further live experiments.)

slumped
↓

We were walking past the library when I spotted Veronica. She was slumped on a beanbag staring out of the window. I knew that she must have been really upset for Miss Crumble to have let her sit on her own instead of being in class.

I didn't understand why, though. Having foam on your school uniform isn't half as bad as what just happened to Poppy. Still, we knew Veronica wouldn't usually get so upset about silly stuff like this, so we decided to go and talk to her.

"It's OK," Poppy said. "I'm fine now, no more foaming!"

"What? Oh," Veronica said. She looked as if she might start to cry again. "It wasn't that—it was all the laughing. I can't be cheerful. Not after what happened last night, not after . . ."

I saw Violet raise an eyebrow. This sounded interesting and mysterious.

mystery eyebrow

"What happened?" I said.
"You know, we are trained detectives. We could help."

Veronica's expression changed. "Of course! You might be able to find them for me—I should have asked you this morning, but I'm not thinking straight. Since they . . . they're GONE!" she spluttered.

Wow! A missing person case. These are totally advanced.

"Who is gone, Veronica?" I said seriously.
"Tell us exactly what happened."

## EYEWITNESS REPORT:
## VERONICA SPENT, AGE 9

slinky

### SUNDAY

**9:30 PM:** Veronica has been allowed to stay up late to groom her three Persian cats, Minky, Binky,

minky

Binky

and Slinky. Their coats need to be in top condition to defend their Best Cat in Show title at the Puddleford Festival. (They've won joint first prize at the festival for three years running, and lots of other cat competitions.)

**9:45 PM:** After filling their bowls with cat treats, Veronica heads upstairs to bed.

### MONDAY

**3:00 AM:** Veronica wakes after a terrible dream about her cats going wild, meowing, and tearing up the pet marquee at the Puddleford Festival.

**3:10 AM:** Telling herself it was a silly dream, Veronica drifts back to sleep. The cats would never destroy a marquee. They are really lazy and can't even be bothered going into the backyard some days.

**7:00 AM:** Veronica is awoken by a scream. It's coming from downstairs and sounds like her mom. Veronica races to see what's happened.

Veronica's mom

**7:03 AM:** Standing in the doorway of the kitchen, Veronica can't believe the chaos. There are cat treats all over the floor, cat beds torn apart, and dishes smashed. There is no sign of Minky, Binky, and Slinky.

**7:04 AM:** Veronica's dad breaks the news that he found the kitchen door wide open and he thinks Minky, Binky, and Slinky have somehow escaped. This is worse than Veronica's nightmare; much worse.

**7:05 AM:** Veronica's mom shouts that the only explanation is that the cats have been catnapped. She is also really mad because Veronica's dad forgot to lock the kitchen door last night.

unlocked!

**7:06 AM:** Veronica realizes she probably did hear the cats going wild and that's why she had the nightmare. She searches the backyard, calling her cats' names, but it's no good. Her lovely pets are gone.

**8:30 AM:** At school, Miss Crumble says Veronica can take as much time out as she needs. (That's why she was sitting in the front row in assembly.) Veronica doesn't know how she'll make it through the day—until the Mystery Girls offer to help, that is.

## NEW MYSTERY TO SOLVE:

catnapper?

What happened to Minky, Binky, and Slinky last night? Have they really been catnapped? Missing cats just got lots more interesting!

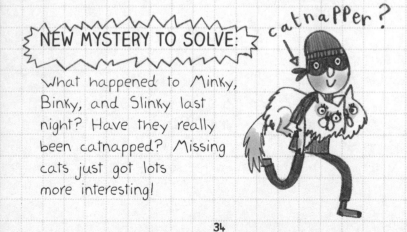

Veronica's ↓ house

# 4:00 PM
# 12 SPRINGSIDE AVENUE,
# VERONICA'S BACKYARD

We went to Veronica's after school to search
for clues.

Veronica's mom has been too upset to clean up the
mess in the kitchen because, when she reported
the suspected catnapping, Detective Sparks from
Puddleford Police said that it sounded far-fetched
and the cats had probably escaped when the
unlocked back door was blown open by the wind.

Blown
← open

Shocking! Not even visiting the scene of a suspected crime is what The Young Super Sleuth's Handbook calls shoddy detective work.

We have inspected the back door— it's far too heavy to have blown open in the wind. No, the way the cats vanished seems extremely fishy, and not just because there are smelly sardine cat treats all over the floor. When Veronica went to answer the phone, we started talking.

"If we could find a ransom note, saying, 'I want a squillion dollars or you'll never see your cats again,' we might be able to trace it back to the catnapper," said Poppy.

meow!

ransom note

"The Young Super Sleuth's Handbook says finding a ransom note is a strong sign of a kidnapping. I'm sure it's the same with catnappings," Violet said. "But I did think there would be some footprints or something too. Are we sure this is a catnapping?"

Hmmm. It could be that there isn't a ransom note because the catnapper wants to keep the cats to win competitions, but Violet does have a point. We need to make sure we are following the right line of inquiry* before we decide what to do next.

*LINE OF INQUIRY: When you focus your investigation around one main suspicion. It's important to get this right or you might miss important clues because you aren't looking in the right place.

"You're right, Violet," I said. "We should stick to the Young Super Sleuth procedure and consider all possible explanations."

## LOGICAL EXPLANATION ONE:

Minky, Binky, and Slinky felt really energetic after eating the cat treats Veronica left out and took themselves out for a walk.

energetic

But Veronica says her cats are really lazy. Also, even though the back door was left unlocked, Veronica's mom is certain it was shut when they went to bed. Cats can't open doors on their own. Can they?

## LOGICAL EXPLANATION TWO:

The bad dream Veronica had caused her to sleepwalk into the kitchen, where she spooked the cats. (When Poppy sleepwalked at my birthday sleepover she looked like a zombie.) Minky, Binky, and Slinky escaped through the kitchen door, which Veronica opened in her sleep.

But Veronica said she has never ever sleepwalked in her whole life.

## LOGICAL EXPLANATION THREE:

Minky, Binky, and Slinky were taken by a crazed catnapper who wants to use them to win prizes or to hold them to ransom because they are valuable, award-winning, pedigree cats.

VERDICT: A deliberate triple catnapping does seem to fit with the chaos left behind in the kitchen and explain why the door was found open. Whatever happened, the cats did not go willingly. The search for Binky, Minky, and Slinky starts here. (Or it would do if we knew where to begin looking.)

The Young Super Sleuth's Handbook says raising awareness can lead to new clues. We are heading back to HQ to make posters asking witnesses to come forward. Sometimes people see odd things but don't realize they are important until they hear about an investigation.

# 6:00 PM
# MYSTERY GIRLS HQ, BEANBAG AREA,
# MAKING CATNAPPER AWARENESS POSTERS

All this talk of catnapping made me remember that actually I hadn't seen Watson since he ran away yesterday. There was no sign of him at HQ, where he usually likes to sleep on the beanbag, and in the kitchen his bowl of cat food was untouched. Mom, Dad, and Arthur haven't seen him either.

Before I start getting worried, I have to remind myself this isn't the first time Watson has wandered off and it is probably nothing to do with Veronica's missing cats. Watson once stayed out all night and most of the next day after Arthur covered his fur in hair clips while he was sleeping. This is the same sort of situation.

hair clips

"Stealing somebody's pets is such a horrible thing to do," Violet said. "We've got to find Veronica's cats. I hope that somebody comes forward with information."

"We should see if there is anyone taking the pet competitions really seriously this year," Poppy said. "He could be a suspect."

"Definitely," I said. "We'll put the posters up in places cat lovers will easily spot them, like outside Paws and Claws (the vet), and Fluff 'n' Feathers (pet shop), and on the Pet Lovers' Club bulletin board at school."

We can't do anything else until tomorrow,
but I'm really pleased with what we managed
to make this evening. Watson and Henry are
probably on their way back now, but in the
slim likelihood that they aren't, I've added their
details to the poster too.

# WARNING: SUSPECTED CATNAPPER ACTIVITY!

HAVE YOU SEEN THESE PEDIGREE PERSIAN CATS?

minky

Binky

slinky

We are also looking for these cats.

(They are probably in a garden shed or something.)

WATSON

Last seen wearing fake mustache.

HENRY, orange. Glitzy collar.

If you have further information, please contact the Mystery Girls.

# Tuesday
# April 21st

Totally prepared to rescue Minky, Binky, and Slinky from the clutches of deranged catnapper. (Could be exciting!)

## 12:45 PM
## PUDDLEFORD ELEMENTARY, CAFETERIA

I couldn't think straight while we were putting up
our posters on the way to school this morning. Last
night, Watson didn't come home—again! He's never
stayed away for two whole nights before. Further
news of missing cats is really making me worry.

We've been inundated* with weird reports. The
Young Super Sleuth's Handbook says you need to
be prepared to wait days for new leads, so this type
of response is usually unheard of.

*INUNDATED: When tons of stuff
happens at once and you are like—
WHOA! All this new information
is making my brain explode.

Exploding
brain

## MISSING CAT REPORTS

**CAT:** Muffin, long–haired gray and white with distinctive white tail
**OWNER:** Lucy North (6th grade)

muffin →

## DETAILS OF DISAPPEARANCE:

Muffin was curled up in his usual position on the end of her bed when Lucy went to sleep. This morning he was gone. This was strange, as Muffin usually snoozes until lunchtime. In the downstairs bathroom, Lucy found an entire pack of twelve toilet paper rolls shredded. The window was wide open and there was no sign of Muffin anywhere. After seeing our posters, Lucy suspects Muffin may have put up a struggle before finally being snatched and carried away.

12 toilet paper rolls!

**CAT:** Ethel, fluffy and white with black patch on chest
**OWNER:** Mrs. Bushell (3rd grade teacher)

## DETAILS OF DISAPPEARANCE:

Mrs. Bushell was awoken at 2 AM by a screeching sound. She raced downstairs and found the cat flap had been torn off. She heard Ethel's frantic meowing fading into the night. Mrs. Bushell ran into the dark street, but Ethel was gone.

Ethel

Gingernut

**CAT:** Gingernut, orange and brown tabby cat
**OWNER:** Joel Stetson (3rd grade)

## DETAILS OF DISAPPEARANCE:

Gingernut was last seen at bedtime, fast asleep on the sofa. This morning, the sofa cushions were found ripped and scattered around the living room. The patio doors (thought to be locked) were ajar.

**OTHER DISAPPEARANCES:** Though there is no evidence of a struggle, the following cats have not returned home for a worrying length of time.

owned by Sandy Turner, 5th grade.

Cat of Jessica Watkin's, 4th grade.

Jinx: missing two days.

Dave: Last seen yesterday morning.

Penny Bolt, 4th grade.

Mr. Socks: gune three days.

Smokey: failed to return home last night.

fluffkin fluffles: didn't return home last night.

Mr. Jones. (caretaker.)

Miss Trunket. (teaching assistant.)

Colin: Not seen since Saturday!

Sam Meek, 1st grade.

**VERDICT:** Some reports of forced entry and signs of a struggle carry the hallmark of catnapping. But there is an alarming number of other cats, including Watson and Henry, who have simply not returned home. We think that the incidents are connected and that our suspicions about there being a catnapper at work are most certainly correct. None of the cats who are now missing are pedigree show cats—if the catnapper doesn't want the cats for competitions, what does he want with them?

C A T N A P P E R
ALERT

We are now investigating: **A KITTY CALAMITY\***.

**\*CALAMITY:** When something goes disastrously wrong, like lots of cats disappearing and when you can't even get excited about a new mystery because you've realized that your own talented detective cat has probably been catnapped too.

CATNAPPED!

Missing Cat
Total: 17

## 1:45 PM
## MISS CRUMBLE'S CLASSROOM, PIONEERS
## OF PUDDLEFORD PROJECT TIME

Lunchtime was crazy—we took another five
reports from people whose cats have gone missing!
By the time we'd finished, when all I wanted was to
have an emergency Mystery Girls meeting, we had
to go back to class to start our inventions workshop
with Horatio.

Horatio arrived wearing
a ridiculous-looking invention
on his head. It looked as
if he'd taped some
tubes and bottles of
lemonade together.

After what happened yesterday, I wasn't sure Horatio would be able to help us make the sort of exciting detective inventions that we are interested in.

"I need to make sure my mouth is flushed out to suppress the foaming action of last night's new batch of toothpaste. Only a slight hitch with my adjustments to the formula, and nothing I can't fix," Horatio said to our class, before slurping from one of the tubes dangling from his head.

He carried on talking about toothpaste for a long time so I decided to write a note to Poppy and Violet.

After school, let's check out the locations missing cats were last seen. The catnapper might come back to take a cat he spotted on his last visit, or he might have left some clues behind. Mariella Mystery x

Mom wants me home by 6 PM for dinner, and catnapper seems to be active at night. Also, what if we get catnapped too? I don't like this! Violet x

Search after school sounds cool. Let's go! But what idea shall we pick for our final invention? I like Lunch Launcher design best. Poppy x

I can't concentrate on anything else. And, Violet, stop worrying. You'd have to be a cat to get catnapped and you aren't. Mariella x

Our note-passing was interrupted by Horatio, who was striding around waving his arms.

"Good ideas don't happen when you're sitting at a desk," Horatio said. "Let's get up and DANCE! I always listen to music while I work—it helps the creative juices flow!"

Horatio beamed, and turned on some loud music.

51

It was really stupid, but I could tell by the expression on Miss Crumble's face that we all had to join in.

"As you are moving, think about your inventions—you might already have an idea, but what will make a difference to the world?" Horatio shouted. "Tell the person next to you!"

meow

"Oh, I don't know," Poppy said, waggling her arms. "Maybe a can of cat food that meows when a catnapper is nearby?"

She was only joking, but it made perfect sense.

"Never mind the control panel or the Lunch Launcher. What we need are inventions to help us solve this case!" I said.

I was a little surprised to find that Horatio was right. The dancing did help. Once I got into it, I stopped worrying about Watson as much and that meant I could think of inventions to help find him and solve the mystery.

Horatio thinks our ideas are really good and was totally shocked when we told him about the Kitty Calamity.

## OUR INVENTION IDEAS:

### THE KITTY SPINNER BY ME:
Spinning cat toys will grab the attention of catnapped cats so we can evacuate them to safety.

battery-powered fan

fishy smell

tuna

papier-mâché

### THE FRAGRANT FISHY BY POPPY:
Device that blows fishy smells into the air from an open can of tuna inside, attracting missing cats close enough for rescue.

### COZY-CAT STROKING MITT BY VIOLET:
Comforting stroking mitts that calm nervous cats down and protect people with allergies.

fake lab
(made by Miss Crumble)

inventions

WEAR SAFETY GOGGLES

THIS WAY UP

## 2:45 PM
## MISS CRUMBLE'S CLASSROOM,
## FAKE MAD SCIENTIST'S LAB AREA

We need to be catnapper detectors (like that cat food invention Poppy thought of). That's why we've been

catnapper
- - - - ▷
detector

working on suspect profiles to help us figure out who this deranged individual is likely to be and why he wants so many cats.

With this information, we've got a better chance of picking the catnapper out in a crowd. (If the catnapper is still in Puddleford and hasn't run away somewhere with all the cats, that is.)

## SUSPECT PROFILES

### SUSPECT ONE: CRAZILY COMPETITIVE ABOUT CATS

Wants his cat to win BIG at the Puddleford Festival on Saturday and is intent on removing all the other competition— not just the big prize-winners like Slinky, Minky, and Binky. We have asked around and none of the other cat owners know anyone who is into cat competitions. It doesn't mean he isn't out there, though.

### SUSPECT TWO: "GO AWAY, KITTY!" CAT HATER

Dislikes cats so much he has decided to steal all the cats in Puddleford. Reasons for not liking cats include cats pooing on flowers, cats sneaking into houses for food, and cats yowling in the night. We have to hope this isn't what we are dealing with and that the cats are still alive and well.

cat poo

## SUSPECT THREE: FISHY DEALER

A rogue pet shop owner is snatching the cats so he can sell already house-trained pets to the unsuspecting public.

The Young Super Sleuth's Handbook says that even nice people can hide terrible secrets but I'm fairly sure Mrs. Finn at Fluff 'n' Feathers isn't involved.

Another, more sinister, pet shop owner could have taken the cats to pet shops miles from Puddleford where nobody will recognize their fluffy little faces. It will be really difficult to solve the case if this has happened because by the time Mom has driven us to pet shops all over the country the missing cats may have already been sold.

Sinister pet shop owner

## SUSPECT FOUR: FELINE FANCIER

Loves cats so much she is catnapping other people's pets. Could be a crazy, old cat lady, like Mrs. Pavlova who lives on my street. This wouldn't be so bad, because at least all the missing cats would be well looked after and probably still close by.

<u>VERDICT</u>: No cat is safe. We can only speculate* as to the motive of the catnapper, but we hope this awareness will help us not to miss crucial or innocent-seeming pieces of evidence. Like a nice old lady carrying a big bag and waving cat treats around. Hopefully we'll see something suspicious that will lead us to the missing cats right after school.

suspicious

**\*SPECULATE:** When you can only guess what is going on because a case is so weird.

57

MISSING CATS: 23

## 5:15 PM
## CORNER OF BLOSSOM LANE
## AND PEAR TREE AVENUE

Apart from the missing cat poster of
Mrs. Bushell's cat Ethel on the lamp post
next to us, everything seems quiet and
normal. But it isn't. Before we even left
school to start our search for clues we
had to add another six furry faces to
our "Suspected Catnapped" list.

In the playground, we overheard a
group of moms talking about their
missing cats. We asked them to tell us
the details and now all I can think about
is how many more cats might have been
taken that we don't know about yet.
This is getting worse!

MISSING

HAVE YOU SEEN
THIS CAT?

As we walked around Puddleford, I kept hoping we'd spot Watson sitting in somebody's front yard, completely fine and un-catnapped. We didn't, though, and we didn't see anyone acting suspiciously either.

But we did make one breakthrough! We've just finished marking the locations the cats were last seen on a map and a totally disturbing pattern has been revealed.

It looks as if, so far, all the missing cats have disappeared from the same part of Puddleford! We are calling this:

## THE CORNER OF CAT-ASTROPHE.

We chose this name because it sounds much more serious than Calamity Corner. (Poppy said that sounded too much like one of those pet play centers you can buy, so your cat can have fun while you are out—and there is nothing fun about this corner.)

PREPARE FOR TERROR!

## 7:15 PM
## MY ROOM, 22 SYCAMORE AVENUE,
## CONDUCTING SURVEILLANCE

When I got home, the first thing I did was look for Watson again, just in case I'd somehow missed a place he could be hiding. But there is still no sign of him.

Arthur is downstairs being all hysterical and dramatic. I don't need him carrying on about it. I know that the longer Watson stays away the more likely it is that he has been catnapped. It got really bad when Mom said we were having fish sticks for dinner.

fish sticks

"I can't eat them!" Arthur sobbed. "They remind me too much of Watson. He loves fish sticks!"

I'm totally upset too, but if I let myself think about Watson, my Mystery Senses go all wonky and I get worried that we'll never solve the case and he'll be gone forever. Then it gets worse and I start thinking stuff like—what if the catnapper has sold all the cats to a cat food factory where they will be forced to test really disgusting flavors of cat food? Or what if the cats have been shaved so their fur can be used to make fluffy cushion covers? The catnapper must be crazy to snatch so many cats, so who knows what he is capable of?

disgusting

SHAVED!

heart-shaped cushion

small cushion

I came upstairs to try and think logically, but it's impossible.

First, I noticed that I'd sat on a lump under my blankets. For a moment I thought we'd been wrong and that Watson had been hiding in my bed the whole time. But when I pulled back the covers, all I found was one of Arthur's fluffy kitten slippers with a note attached to it.

I thought you might want to HUG this tonight. I'll be hugging the other one. LOVE and CUDDLES ARTHUR xxx

I was about to go crazy with Arthur because he knows he isn't allowed in my room, and those stupid kitten slippers are probably the whole reason Watson ran away into the hands of the catnapper in the first place. But then I decided I should probably give him a break.

kitty confusion

He is so small and annoying that his brain can't handle situations like this. I'm a trained detective and I can't think straight, so Arthur must be in a state of severe kitty-induced confusion. (And actually, without Watson around, it might be nice to have something to cuddle tonight.)

I can't believe Mom and Dad wouldn't let me go on a late-night patrol of the Corner of CAT-astrophe. Dad said lots of people have been calling the *Puddleford Gazette* (where he works). He thinks it might not be safe out there.

At least I live inside the Corner of CAT-astrophe, so I might be able to spot weird activity from my window. All I can do is keep watch and try not to look at Watson's kitty gym. He loves the swinging fish with a bell on it the most. When he gets home I'll never get annoyed with him playing with it while I'm trying to sleep again.

SOB!

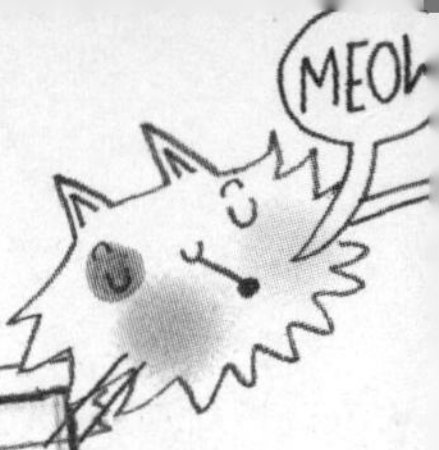


# Wednesday April 22nd

Where are you, Watson?

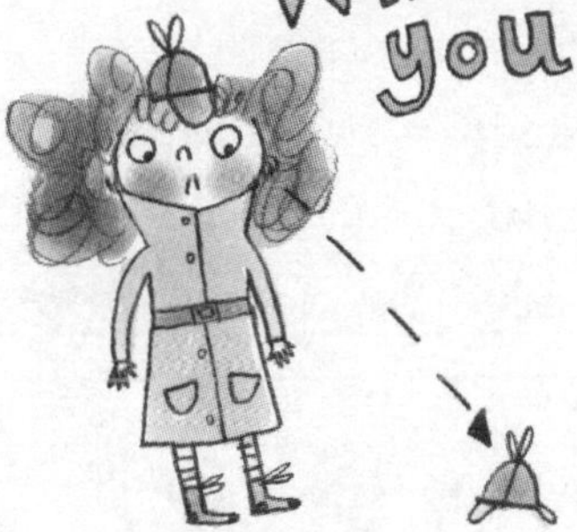

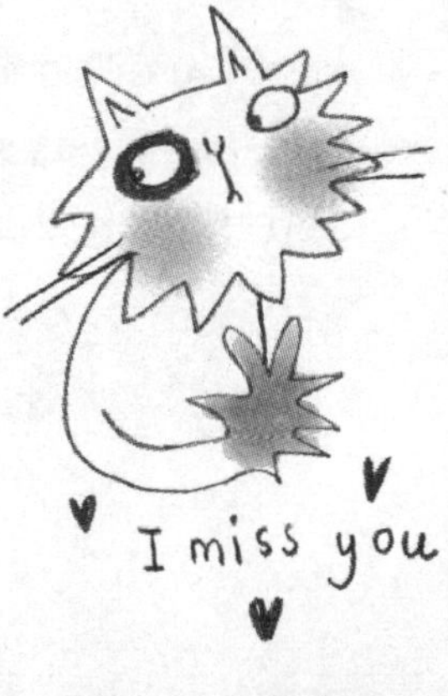

1:30 AM
MY BEDROOM, IN SHOCK.
POSSIBLE CATNAPPING ACTIVITY ALERT!

I can't believe what has JUST happened.

I must have fallen asleep while monitoring
the street for suspicious activity. The next thing
I knew, I was having a horrible nightmare.
Watson was yowling because he was being
forced to wear a hideous fluffy, pink,
knitted dress by a totally crazy
old cat lady catnapper, and
I couldn't save him
because I was stuck
in a giant ball of yarn.

CRAZY

I woke up tangled in the blankets between the bed and the windowsill. The crazy meowing and yowling carried on. It took me a few seconds to realize that it was coming from outside.

I grabbed my Young Super Sleuth binoculars and scanned the street. Sycamore Avenue was silent and still. I thought I must have still been dreaming, but then it came again.

MeeeeoowwwWWWW!
MeeeeeoooW MeeeeeeoooooW!

Further along the street, under the flickering beam of a street lamp, two cats sprinted onto Sycamore Avenue. A chubby black and white cat and a small tabby kitten. They looked frightened, as if they were running away from something terrible. I couldn't see anyone chasing them, but the catnapper could have been just around the corner.

As they ran past my house, the chubby cat let out an ear-splittingly loud screech.

MeeOOOWWWW

aarrggghhh!

I'm not telling anyone it was so scary that I almost fell off the bed again when I heard it. But my detective brain said that, no matter how spooked I was, this might be an excellent opportunity to apprehend* the catnapper.

*APPREHEND: To catch somebody, like an evil catnapper, and restrain him until you can decide what to do next, because you haven't thought that far ahead yet.

I leaped off the bed and out onto the landing. Then tripped over Mom's knitting bag and fell through Arthur's bedroom door.

**CRASH!**

"AAAaaaERRRRRGHHHHH!" Arthur screeched. "It's the catnapper!" He started launching all his toys at me.

ARGH!

After that I had no chance of persuading Mom and Dad I needed to go outside and chase the catnapper. They were really annoyed and made me go back to bed.

# Unbelievable.

So now I'm stuck sitting here when the catnapper could have run right past my house! What did he do to make those cats SO terrified? I can only hope that they got away safely.

## 9:45 AM
## MISS CRUMBLE'S CLASSROOM (INVENTION MAKING SESSION WITH HORATIO)

**IMPORTANT DEVELOPMENT ALERT!**

I'm supposed to be working on my Kitty Spinner—
there are only three days until the Puddleford
Festival and finishing it to help solve the case is
more essential than ever—but I need to write this
down. I've hardly had any time to discuss what I
saw last night with Poppy and Violet because this
morning we've had reports of sightings of some of
the missing cats—three of them!

# CASE REPORT: MISSING CAT SIGHTINGS

**WITNESS:** Josie from next door
**CAT:** Henry

Josie

**7:15 AM:** While getting cleaned up, Josie spots what she thinks is a scruffy stray cat walking along the backyard fence.
She looks closer and realizes it is actually her beloved Henry.

**7:16 AM:** Josie races outside, screaming Henry's name. Henry stares at Josie as if he doesn't know who she is, then jumps into the yard next door. (On the other side, not mine.)

**7:17 AM:** Still in her nightgown, Josie scales the fence, but it's too late. Henry is already gone.

SCRUFFY

**WITNESS:** Horatio Tweed
**CAT:** Slinky (one of Veronica's cats)

**8:05 AM:** As Horatio leaves for school from his home on Blossom Lane, a cat with matted fur (that we now think was Slinky) darts across his path.

slinky?

**8:06 AM:** Knowing it might be one of the missing cats, Horatio tries to get Slinky's attention with a tuna sandwich from his lunchbox. Slinky hisses and bolts over the hedge.

tuna

**WITNESS:** Mrs. Bushell
**CAT:** Ethel

**8:30 AM:** Poppy overhears the school receptionist telling Miss Twist that Mrs. Bushell had called to say she won't be coming in because she is sick with worry after almost running over her missing cat, Ethel, on Pear Tree Avenue.

**8:32 AM:** The school receptionist explains that Ethel wandered into the road in front of Mrs. Bushell's car. Ethel was in a daze, and her usually white fur was gray. Mrs. Bushell slammed on her brakes, but Ethel hissed at her and raced off.

**8:33 AM:** Miss Twist calls Mrs. Bushell back to tell her that almost running over your cat is no excuse for taking off from school.

**VERDICT:** We believe these cats managed to escape from the catnapper and are so traumatized by their experience that they are refusing to go anywhere near humans—even their owners.

TRAUMATIZED

The location of the sightings suggests that wherever the cats escaped from must be close by. On the one hand, this is a good thing, because they aren't far from home, but on the other, this makes the whole thing worse, because the catnapper is hiding the cats right under our noses and we still don't have a clue where!

**NOTE:** The only thing we know is that the cats all look a mess. This suggests they are being held somewhere dirty.

## POSSIBLE CAT HIDING LOCATIONS:

### AN OLD ABANDONED WAREHOUSE:
I've never noticed one of these in Puddleford.

### A DARK CELLAR:
There must be lots of houses with cellars in Puddleford—it will take weeks to search them all!

DARK CELLAR

### PUDDLEFORD DUMPSTER: Always busy—would somebody risk hiding cats there?

### IN A WASTE BIN OR GARBAGE CAN:
I'm sure cats would make lots of noise if they were stuck in a garbage can, so surely somebody would have noticed.

MEOW

**Argh!** I'm trying not to think about Watson being stuck in any of those locations.

MISSING CATS: 53

**12:35 PM
LUNCHTIME, PUDDLEFORD ELEMENTARY,
NEXT TO PET LOVERS' CLUB BULLETIN BOARD**

The Pet Lovers' bulletin board is overflowing with missing cat stories. We were getting so many reports that we told people to post the details of new disappearances here.

Among the fluffy faces of the lost cats are photos of the black and white cat and the kitten I saw from my bedroom window last night. They belong to Cece Huffwell from 3rd grade. Egg (chubby cat) and Chip (the kitten) went missing in another suspected catnapped-through-the-cat-flap incident in the early hours of this morning.

FLAPPY CAT

catnapped! →

"I do not like this! The Corner of CAT-astrophe is getting bigger," Violet said. "Soon Puddleford will be one huge catastrophic cat-free zone!"

Violet is right. We've been marking each new disappearance on our map and the area is expanding.

"Maybe so many cats going missing is a good thing," I said. "The sightings today suggest the cats are still in Puddleford. If that is the case it's going to be much more difficult to conceal them. Whoever is behind this can't hide his furry little secret forever."

Even though things seem terrible I think we've got a good chance of finding the cats after school. We'll keep our eyes open for a messy house with loud meowing coming from its cellar. Or maybe an abandoned warehouse we've never noticed before.

FLUFF 'N' FEATHERS PET SHOP

**6:15 PM
OUTSIDE FLUFF 'N' FEATHERS, PUDDLEFORD MAIN STREET**

Searching the whole of the Corner of CAT-astrophe will take days (it's really big), so we focused our attention on the locations the cats have been sighted.

Walking down Pear Tree Avenue and Sycamore Avenue (my road), there was no sign of any missing cats, messy houses, abandoned warehouses, or anything else suspicious. We all got excited when Violet spotted a huge dumpster outside a house on Blossom Lane, but it was full of furniture. Not cats.

PUDDLEFORD DUMPSTER

The only other thing we saw was lots of worried
owners searching for their cats.

"Fluffkin Fluffles? Fluffy? Fluffles!
Are you out there?"

"GingerNuUUUT! "

"MUFFIN! MUFFIN! MUFFIIIIN!"

"If only I'd managed to finish the Fragrant Fishy
sooner, we could be using it to draw the cats out
from wherever they're hidden," Poppy said.

Every lamp post we walked past had at least
one missing cat notice stuck to it, sometimes more.
It felt as if the eyes of the lost cats of Puddleford
were watching us miserably,
saying, "Why haven't you
rescued us yet?"

← LOST
CATS

PLEASE
rescue
us!

By the time we got back to my house, Poppy and Violet looked as fed up as I felt. But The Young Super Sleuth's Handbook says remaining positive is essential if you want to solve a case.

"It's only a matter of time," I said. "I'm sure the catnapper is bound to slip up soon."

"Actually, I just thought. What if the catnapper has been in to Fluff 'n' Feathers to buy hundreds of cans of cat food?" said Poppy, looking happier. "The shop will be closed now but we could ask tomorrow!"

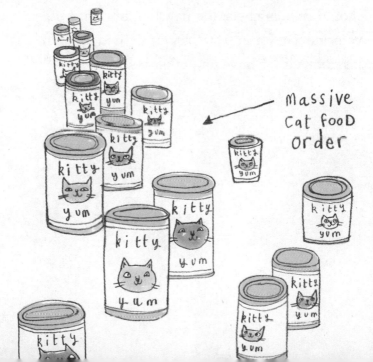

massive
Cat fooD
order

"We should check the veterinarian too," Violet said. "The catnapper might have registered fifty-three cats under new names."

Hmmm. I'm glad that Violet and Poppy are thinking of useful things we can do, but I'm not sure the catnapper would be that stupid. He must know people would start asking questions about big orders of cat food and one person suddenly getting lots of new pet cats.

The Young Super Sleuth's Handbook says to explore every possibility, though, so I suppose we should double-check the pet shop and visit the veterinarian for any suspicious activity, just in case. It's not as if we have any other leads.

determined

MISSING CATS: 65

## 5:30 PM
## OUTSIDE PAWS AND CLAWS VETERINARIAN'S OFFICE, PUDDLEFORD TOWN CENTER

It's been a really stressful day. Lots more missing cat reports and the Kitty Spinner's spinner flew across the classroom when I tested it.

Horatio said not to worry and that I'll definitely get it sorted before the festival, but I really hoped I might be able to use it to tempt a cat out from its hiding place tonight. I wanted a back-up plan because I wasn't sure our visit to the pet shop and veterinarian was going to reveal any new clues, but I was wrong.

When we got to Fluff 'n' Feathers, Mrs. Finn told us she'd been really worried about the catnapper and that she was relieved not to have any kittens for sale in the shop at the moment. She also told us she'd been awoken at around midnight a couple of times this week by the horrible sound of distressed cats yowling.

It was as I suspected—when we asked if any customers had ordered enough food for 65 cats, Mrs. Finn said no. I was starting to feel frustrated. Luckily, our visit to Paws and Claws was more interesting.

We arrived just before the office closed. The waiting room was quiet, apart from a lady waiting to be seen with her Chihuahua, and two veterinary nurses chatting behind the reception desk. My Mystery Senses picked up right away that one of the nurses was anxious. Her badge said her name was Rachel.

anxious

Rachel

"I'm not looking forward to the night shift. Not after what happened," Rachel said. "Those cats were crazy. If there's even a sniff of anything weird tonight, I'm going home."

Poppy nudged me. I knew what she was thinking. We needed to know about any strange cat-related activity—and this definitely sounded strange.

"We are detectives investigating the Missing Cats of Puddleford. Would you mind if we asked you a few questions?" I said, stepping forward.

## EYEWITNESS REPORT: RACHEL RUFO, VETERINARY NURSE AT PAWS AND CLAWS

## WEDNESDAY (EARLY HOURS OF MORNING)

**12:45 AM:** Rachel checks on patients staying on the Overnight Ward. A black cat named Terry, who has a broken leg, and a Siamese cat named Pearl, with an eye infection, are both fast asleep in their crates.

Bandage

Plaster cast

**12:55 AM:** Noting that Barry the basset hound appears comfortable, after surgery to remove the plastic dog bone he ate, and Errol the hamster is recovering well after eating a bag of cotton balls, Rachel decides her midnight tea break is well overdue.

**1:20 AM:** Rachel is halfway through her cup of tea and third triple chocolate finger cookie when there is a disturbing noise from the ward. MEAArrrggghhHH! Whoever is making that terrible sound must need medical attention.

**1:21 AM:** Rachel races to the ward, swings open the door, and gasps.

**1:22 AM:** Terry is throwing himself against the crate and screeching—MEEARRRAGGGIIOOOW! Pearl is hissing and has shredded her cushion to pieces.

**1:23 AM:** Before Rachel can do anything, a crate door crashes to the floor and she sees a flash of black fur—Terry has escaped. He darts toward the back of the Overnight Ward, his plaster cast flying behind him.

**1:24 AM:** In all her years of working with animals, Rachel has never witnessed a cat cling to a door handle with its teeth and swing around as if trying to open it. Pearl launches herself at her crate door for the final time. The crate tips forward and topples over, releasing the door catch—and Pearl.

**1:25 AM:** Suddenly there is a click and the Overnight Ward door opens into the darkness. Terry and Pearl tear away across the parking lot.

**1:26 AM:** Running after them, Rachel sees Terry and Pearl are at the top of Main Street, prowling outside Sunny Places travel agents— with two other cats! All four cats yowl at the same time—MEOOOGGGHHHHIOOW—then sprint down Pear Tree Avenue and disappear into the night.

**1:28 AM:** It's the weirdest thing Rachel has ever experienced and she feels quite scared. When Barry the basset hound howls from inside Rachel decides she can't abandon her night shift, not when sick animals need her, so she goes back to Paws and Claws.

This is an artist's impression of the cats Rachel saw with Terry and Pearl. ➡️

**VERDICT:** WEIRD ALERT! Rachel didn't see a catnapper, so why were Terry and Pearl so desperate to escape? And why did they run away with those other cats? We're sure this can't just be a random case of two crazy cats—not when there is so much other cat madness happening.

**NOTE:** Rachel told us Terry and Pearl seemed to be in a trance, like when you give a cat catnip*.

Catnip toy

**\*CATNIP:** A plant that humans can't smell but that cats love the smell of. It is often put into cat toys. Could Pearl and Terry sense something like this that was driving them crazy?

cat nip

## 6:45 PM
## MYSTERY GIRLS HQ, EMERGENCY MYSTERY
## GIRL TEAM MEETING

We'd been looking for new evidence, but Rachel's story seems to have made things lots more confusing.

The two cats at the vet seemed to go completely crazy all by themselves. There was no sign of anyone trying to steal the cats, and the crazed screeching noises Rachel described sound VERY similar to the noises Egg and Chip were making when I saw them on Tuesday night. Now that I think of it, Egg and Chip were running down my street at exactly the same time the cats went crazy at the veterinarian's office!

egg and
chip

Could whatever made Terry and Pearl go crazy
also have affected Egg and Chip? Were all the
other missing cats acting the same way? Something
Rachel had described was making me think that we
needed to consider it.

"We thought the mess the other missing cats
left behind was caused by a struggle with the
catnapper, but could it have been caused by them
trying to escape, like Terry and Pearl?" I said.

CRAZY cats

"But what would make the cats behave like that?"
Violet said. "Was the catnapper doing something
outside to drive them crazy?"

"I don't know," I said. (Because I didn't.) "It could
be that. Or maybe we need to consider other
explanations, just to make sure we aren't missing
anything."

"Um, like what?" Poppy said, pacing up and down HQ.

We've decided to do a review of all the evidence so far. The Young Super Sleuth's Handbook says this can help you look at a case in a new light.

## EXPLANATIONS BASED ON EVIDENCE SO FAR
(Not logical ones, because none of this is logical.)

Explanation One: catnapper is pumping high strength catnip into the air to make the cats run away from home before capturing them. This could be a new technique the catnapper has started using the past few nights so he doesn't have to break into homes.

But why were some sighted this morning, and then again outside the travel agents by Rachel? Did they escape—or were they never catnapped in the first place?

**Explanation Two:** There is no catnapper. There is a giant catnip factory that we don't know about pumping catnip into the air without realizing the strength of the catnip they are producing.

high strength

CATNIP CO.

Surely we'd know if there was a giant catnip factory nearby? And if there were, wouldn't the cats be going crazy all day and not just in the middle of the night?

**Explanation Three:** The cats are being catnapped by aliens who want to make a new species of alien cat people. They are sending messages on a frequency only cats can receive.

No aliens have been sighted, but they could just be invisible or something.

cat alien

alien cat signals

**Explanation Four:** The cats are turning into werecats (a little like werewolves). As soon as it gets dark, a supernatural force turns them from friendly pets into wild, rampaging, crazy cats.

WERECAT!

MUTATING

NORMAL

Nobody has reported being attacked by any werecat-type creatures. Maybe that's because victims have turned into werecats themselves, but I think it's more likely that Violet (who suggested this theory) is letting the spooky undercurrent of this case get to her.

**Explanation Five:** We are totally amateur detectives who are missing a massive clue to tell us how to get to the bottom of the Kitty Calamity!

I'd say this was the most likely explanation so far.

AMATEUR detectives!

93

## 9:20 PM
## MY BEDROOM, MYSTERY DESKS IN DEEP CONCENTRATION

None of our weird theories makes very much sense. But the Young Super Sleuth's Handbook says that even if your brain feels scrambled you still need to come up with a plan. So that's what we did. Or that's what Poppy did while we were staring at the alarming number of missing cat names now marked on the map of the Corner of CAT-astrophe.

(I'm glad I can rely on my fellow Mystery Girls because the more time I spend apart from my trusty sidekick the more my detective brain turns to mush.)

my detective brain

"What if we could track one of the missing cats?" Poppy said. "If we could just find one somehow, it might lead us to where all the missing cats are, or to the catnapper."

It was the best idea any of us had been able to come up with, even if it definitely wasn't as simple as Poppy made it sound.

TRACK
-A-
CAT!

"But none of the owners have had any luck in their searches for the cats and neither have we," Violet added. "I know a few cats were spotted today, but it could take a long time to locate another. We might never find them because soon there could be no cats left in Puddleford."

A Puddleford without cats meant a Puddleford without Watson. That was too awful to think about. But what Violet said made me remember something I'd read in the Young Super Sleuth's Handbook that we haven't had a chance to try before.

"What if we could get everyone working together?" I said. "We should organize a mass search! We'll be able to cover a bigger area and find more clues."

"Actually, that could work, Mariella," Violet said. "I bet there are lots of people who'd help."

We've already started thinking through all the details. I'm sure Miss Crumble will agree to let us hold onto our inventions overnight. (All the finished ones are being entered into the competition after school tomorrow.) She'll understand that a true Pioneer of Puddleford would use her invention to rescue cats.

me, being a Pioneer of PUDDLEFORD

And Poppy says we're sure to solve the case tomorrow night, so we can still put the inventions in as a last-minute entry first thing on Saturday.

We'll split up and each lead a search party* around different areas of the Corner of CAT-astrophe. For all we know, when we were looking yesterday there could have been cat activity happening in another area that we missed.

**\*SEARCH PARTY:** Not a balloons and cake sort of party. It's a group of people working together to find out what has happened to the cats of Puddleford. Once they are found then we can have a less serious party to celebrate! A party where cats are invited because I'm never leaving Watson on his own again once I get him back.

cat cupcakes

Anyway, Dad says if I finish writing a notice about the search party in the next half an hour, he'll make sure it goes in tomorrow's *Puddleford Gazette*. If our plan works, by tomorrow night Watson could be home safely! YES!

# ORGANIZING A MASS SEARCH

You've searched high and low but simply cannot find the clue, suspect, missing person, or pet you are looking for. Why not try organizing a mass search? With more people, the chances of finding what you are looking for are significantly increased.

## A Mass Search Needs . . .

**A STRONG LEADER:** You must be a confident speaker in order to brief search teams. (Use a mega-phone if you don't have a loud voice.)

LISTEN TO ME!

mega LOUD

**RECRUITS:** Willing volunteers who are prepared to leave no stone unturned. (Choose people you can rely on not to miss evidence or tamper with clues.)

I am reliable!

I'll help!

Woooh! A search!

Woof!

**TEAMS:** Split into teams and spread out to cover every inch of a search area. Equip your team with evidence bags and magnifying glasses.

**BASE CAMP:** Set up an area where any objects and clues discovered on the search can be taken for further analysis.

## WARNING

Be prepared with flashlights, spare batteries, warm clothes, and sensible shoes. (No high heels or floaty dresses.)

## TOP TIP

Don't work your team too hard. Provide refreshing tea breaks and give motivational speeches to keep your volunteers inspired. A plate of cookies will give people the energy and determination needed to carry on.

## THINGS TO LOOK OUT FOR ON THE SEARCH

A big hole nobody has noticed.

a BIG hole?

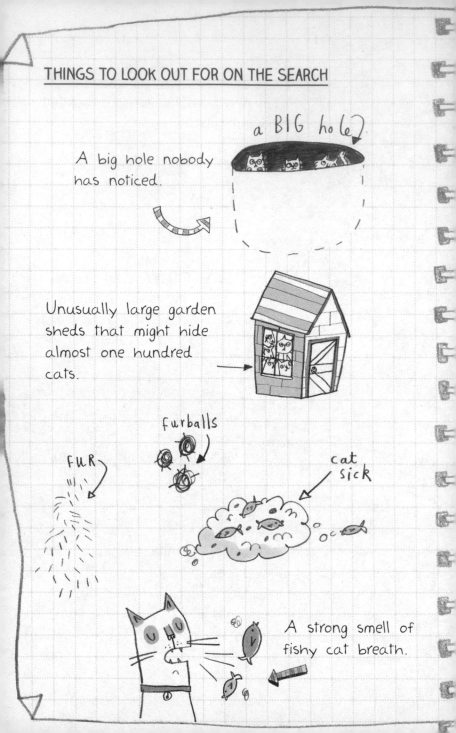

Unusually large garden sheds that might hide almost one hundred cats.

FUR

furballs

cat sick

A strong smell of fishy cat breath.

# Friday
# April 24th

mystery kit is packed for the search

flashlight

evidence bags

cat treats

cat ear headbands

detective breakfast

# 8:05 AM
# BREAKFAST TABLE, MY HOUSE

I hardly slept last night. At 12:02 AM I heard more weird cat noises. This is so frustrating! The cats are so close, but we can't work out where—or why they are acting this way.

Some good news, though. I finished our notice just in time for Dad to send it to the paper. Ideally I'd have liked the search to have been later at night, when the cats seem to be at their craziest, but Mom didn't think we'd get as many people coming if we did that—not when they have to be up early for the Puddleford Festival tomorrow.

# CAT-ASTROPHE IN PUDDLEFORD

Local teacher searches for her cat, Ethel

Unless you haven't left the house in the past few days, you won't have been able to miss that Puddleford is currently in the grip of a Kitty Calamity of epic proportions.

We regret to advise readers that in the last week it is estimated over half of Puddleford's cats appear to have vanished.

The situation is being investigated by local mystery solvers, the Mystery Girls. They suspect this could be the work of a cunning catnapper using strange methods to lure cats away. Other theories include alien abductions and a mystery leak of potent catnip into the atmosphere.

In a strange twist of fate, this year's hotly anticipated Puddleford Festival is sponsored by Kitty Yum Luxury Cat Products.

We asked founder Lizbeth Felange to tell us how she feels about being associated with a town consumed by kitty chaos:

Kitty Yum owner,
Lizbeth Felange

"Puddleford is where my business started, and with these terrible stories of missing cats, I would feel I was letting an old friend down if I pulled out."

Some of you may be concerned to hear that Puddleford Police are not treating the missing cat situation as a priority.

Detective Sparks gives us his insight:

"It is odd that so many cats have vanished at the same time, so I'd urge cat owners to remain vigilant, but my officers will only have time to look into the matter after the festival. People will really moan if the lines for hot dogs aren't monitored for line jumpers because officers are off investigating missing cats."

If you have any theories on what might be behind this startling rise in missing cats, we urge you to contact our news desk on the usual number.

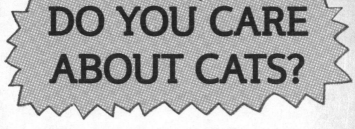

# DO YOU CARE ABOUT CATS?

If the answer is YES, Local Mystery Solvers, the Mystery Girls, urgently need your help.

We are coordinating a mass search of an area known as the Corner of CAT-astrophe for missing cats. With your help we intend to locate a missing cat and track it. We hope this will lead us to much-needed clues and bring a swift end to the Kitty Calamity.

Meet outside the house of Mariella Mystery, 22 Sycamore Avenue, for a pre-search briefing at 7 PM.

(If the answer was no, you don't care about cats, you should go and take a long hard look in the mirror and decide whether you can live with yourself.)

MISSING
CATS: 75

## 12:45 PM
## PUDDLEFORD ELEMENTARY, CAFETERIA

After the advertisement in the *Puddleford Gazette*,
we are expecting a big turn-out for tonight's search.

Horatio has been really helpful. He did a fantastic
job of persuading Miss Crumble that our finished
inventions are more than a school project and
can't be entered into the competition just yet,
because they are needed as ground-breaking
cat rescue devices. He isn't coming on the search
tonight though; he says he's got to work on his final
toothpaste trials before the festival tomorrow.

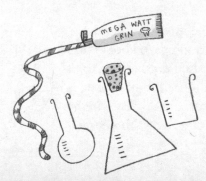
MEGA WATT
GRIN

"Sorry, girls. Mega Watt Grin is almost there and I've just found out that the TV show *Puddleford in Focus* are going to be filming my demonstration!" he said. "I'm hoping the exposure will generate excitement from the big toothpaste companies."

I'm disappointed, but I suppose that even though I'd like Horatio to be the Official Inventor Friend of the Mystery Girls, he can't drop everything and work for us. I'm not sure Mega Watt Grin will ever be perfected, but he's worked so hard on it that he's got to make sure he gives it the best chance of wowing everyone tomorrow.

If he pulls it off, and if we solve the case tonight, we could have a double celebration!

mystery Girl
search outfits

(cat ears to
make cats feel at ease)

## 6:55 PM
## MY HOUSE, SITTING ON WALL
## OF GARDEN

There are already lots of people here—at least
thirty. Hooray! I'm trying to focus on that, rather
than the fact that Arthur has somehow managed
to convince Mom that he has to be on my team.
Poppy and Violet find him far less annoying than I
do and it's vital that I am not distracted in any way,
so I said he needed to go on one of their teams.

"Don't be mean, Mariella," Mom said. "Arthur just
wants to help and he'll be with me the whole time
anyway."

"Yeah, and my invention is going to help us find Watson," Arthur said, proudly holding up what he'd made with Horatio.

googly eyes

yarn

THE MEOW-MEOW LOVE FACE (NONSENSE!)

Ugh. Arthur has been going around showing that stupid thing to everyone. Apparently it's meant to be a friendly cat's face that cats will be drawn to. It looks more like a multi-colored blob of cat poo to me. No wonder his teacher, Mrs. Lovelace, said he didn't have to send it to the festival with the other entries. She must have known it wouldn't win anything.

"What if we uncover something really scary?" Violet said. "Those cats I heard yowling in the middle of the night sounded like they might be werecats."

MEARGH!

WERECAT

"Violet, we've talked about this. It's highly unlikely that this is a werecat problem," I said.

"Just because we haven't heard about any attacks, doesn't mean there haven't been any," Violet said.

"Whatever happens, make sure you don't damage our inventions—we won't have time to remake them before the festival tomorrow," Poppy said.

Honestly, what we need to focus on is the search. Poppy's team is going to the farm and surrounding wasteland. Violet is taking her team to the secret shortcut on Garden Road, and I'm heading toward Leafy Drive. There's a footpath there that hardly ever gets used and would be the perfect hiding place for cats.

This is it. Operation Corner-a-Kitty is Go.

## 9:25 PM
## MY BEDROOM, 22 SYCAMORE AVENUE

I can't believe what just happened. If Arthur had gone in Poppy's or Violet's group like I said he should, we would have solved the case by now. I can barely bring myself to write down the details:

## CASE REPORT:
## OPERATION CORNER-A-KITTY.

**7:05 PM:** After a successful and motivational briefing, the teams depart, calling cats' names as they go. "Fluffkin! Gingernut! WATSON!"

Gingernut!

**7:10 PM:** Heading east along Sycamore Avenue, everything looks normal. My walkie-talkie crackles. I pull it from my pocket and the rest of my team rush to hear what the news is.

**7:11 PM:** Violet's voice fuzzes out: "Mariella? Can you hear me? I don't like this! Are you sure I should be leading a group? Can't your dad do it?" I tell Violet to get a grip and remember her Mystery Girl training.

**7:18 PM:** Walking down Forest Way, Mom calls my name. I spin around, hoping she is alerting me to a cat sighting. She asks if Arthur is with me because she can't see him anywhere. WHAT? Arthur is meant to be with her!

**7:25 PM:** Even though I'm supposed to be in charge, nobody on the search team will listen to me. They are too busy calling Arthur's name and reassuring Mom.

Mom

**7:26 PM:** A crazy cat yowls in the distance. (This is good—it means cats are nearby! It's also weird. The cats have only ever been heard very late at night until now.)

**7:27 PM:** I radio Poppy and Violet to check if they heard the yowl or spotted any cats. The walkie-talkie fuzzes and falls silent. Have Poppy and Violet been attacked by werecats or captured by a deranged catnapper?

ARGH!

**7:28 PM:** I realize Poppy and Violet are probably fine, it's just that the batteries have run out on my walkie-talkie.

POWER POWER

**7:45 PM:** Cat yowls are sounding every few minutes but still no sightings, not that anyone in my group cares. Arthur is still missing.

**8:10 PM:** My search party bumps into Violet's on the corner of Blossom Lane. She is breathless and keeps apologizing. I finally get her to explain and she says she saw Watson, but he ran away. WHAT?

WATSON!

**8:12 PM:** Poppy appears around the corner, with her group—and Arthur! He is being carried by Dad. Mom runs over and starts hugging him. Dad says he thought Mom knew that when we set off Arthur had decided to go in Violet's group because she looked worried and needed back-up more than I did. Arggghhhh!

*yuck*

**8:14 PM:** Poppy says her group saw two cats out on the farm but couldn't keep up with them.

**8:25 PM:** Mom says we should stop the search now because it's dark and everyone is fed up. She also says I am in trouble for shouting at Arthur because it isn't his fault I didn't see any cats. IT IS.

## OPERATION CORNER-A-KITTY OUTCOME:

CONFIRMED SIGHTINGS (GOOD)
TRACKING UNSUCCESSFUL (VERY BAD).

## 10:05 PM
## MY ROOM, 22 SYCAMORE AVENUE

I'm trying to stay positive and not think about the fact that we don't seem to be any closer to figuring out what's going on. Or bringing Watson home.

## POSITIVE THINGS ABOUT THE SEARCH:

1. Plenty of people came.
   (But even with lots of
   help, we didn't track a cat.)

2. I know Watson is alive,
   which is a huge relief.
   I just wish it had been
   me who saw him.

Find me!

3. Spotting more cats who haven't been seen since they first disappeared is a strong indication that others may be close by. (But does this mean they are just spending their time hiding and waiting for night to fall so they can run around Puddleford screeching? Why? I do not get this.)

4. The crazy cat yowling was heard much earlier than on previous nights—so whatever is driving the cats crazy must have been happening at the time of our search. But we didn't see werecats, catnappers, or aliens—or any clues to explain it.

MEARGH!

Before Poppy and Violet went home, I made them tell me every detail of their missing cat sightings, especially Watson's.

"Watson ran past, down the middle of Garden Road. He was such a mess I hardly recognized him," Violet said. "By the time I told the group to follow, he had already disappeared into the secret shortcut."

"Violet's right," said Poppy. "We had no chance. Muffin and Ethel flew out from under a cabbage like furry lightning. And that's not the worst part."

I looked at Poppy, bracing myself for more bad news.

"As I was running," she said, "tuna juice leaked over the Fragrant Fishy's papier-mâché. I'm just hoping it dries out before the festival."

leaky tuna

I know the Fragrant Fishy is important to Poppy, but getting it soggy doesn't seem like that big of a disaster. Not compared to the cats who are stuck out there being crazy or catnapped.

I've let Watson down. If I can't save him, I don't deserve to be a Mystery Girl. Being a detective doesn't feel right without my trusty sidekick.

MEAWoo!*

*cat for HELP ME!

## Working with a Sidekick

With its long hours and heavy workload, mystery-solving can be a lonely occupation. Why not select a sidekick to keep you company and share ideas with?

## Types of Sidekick:

**TRAINEE MYSTERY SOLVER:** Somebody who will say, "Wow! How did you think of that? You are a genius." (An excellent boost for mystery solving confidence. May not be so good at offering advice when you are stuck.)

YOU ARE AMAZING!

**ANIMALS:** Famed for their loyalty and intelligence, sniffer dogs are the traditional detective sidekick. You could also try adopting more unusual animals to help you out.

Ape

Frog

Tortoise

**THE GENIUS INVENTOR:** This person may not have the skills to join you in dramatic mystery situations but can provide high-quality mystery-solving gadgets designed to suit your needs.

## REAL LIFE DETECTIVES: SASSY McFARLANE AND HER NOT-SO-SUPER SIBLING

After nagging from her parents, Sassy McFarlane, three times Young Super Sleuth Of The Year, finally agreed to take on her younger brother, Marcus McFarlane, as her sidekick.

Marcus was not suited to life as a detective. He destroyed evidence by coloring on it with crayons, had tantrums during suspect interrogations, and abandoned suspect surveillance because he had to go to the bathroom.

Sassy fired Marcus and is now rebuilding her mystery-solving career. Don't make the same mistake. Sometimes parents aren't right.

**WARNING**

Yes, this is my detective agency.

A sidekick is supposed to complement your skills, not overshadow them. Beware of sidekicks trying to take over and push you out of your own detective agency.

**10:30 PM**
**MYSTERY GIRLS HQ, LATE-NIGHT EMERGENCY**
**MEETING, (WITH MYSELF BECAUSE POPPY**
**AND VIOLET ARE AT HOME IN BED)**

## TOTALLY AMAZING BREAKTHROUGH
## ALERT.

(Hooray! I don't need to give up being a detective
after all!)

Mom and Dad have gone to bed early after all
the drama so nobody noticed me coming down to
HQ to clear my head. I can always think more like
a detective in here.

120

I was feeling totally useless because I didn't
know what to do next. The Young Super Sleuth's
Handbook says that sometimes you have to hit rock
bottom before you can see your next step clearly—
and, as usual, it was right.

I realized that if Watson could
have seen me, moping around
and feeling sorry for myself, he'd
probably say, "Come on. This is
not the Mariella I know and
enjoy being stroked by—
PULL YOURSELF TOGETHER!"
(If he could talk, that is.)

The Young Super Sleuth's Handbook also says that
if you are stuck you should check your existing
evidence for clues you may have missed.

At first, all I could see were our unanswered questions. Then, as I shuffled through the case file, a piece of paper fluttered out.  It was my sketch of the unknown cats Rachel from Paws and Claws had seen on Tuesday night—the cats she saw running down Peartree Avenue.

It made me think that, actually, even though Poppy and Violet hadn't managed to track the cats they saw, they did see which direction they were headed.

I didn't know whether that was relevant but I started marking their movements on our map of the Corner of CAT-astrophe. As I added more cats, I got that amazing feeling, like when your brain is starting to unscramble a totally complicated problem, like I was piecing together a jigsaw puzzle.

Here's the totally amazing part—all the cats were going the same way!

Watson, Muffin, Gingernut, Terry, Pearl, and the other cats Rachel saw, AND even Egg and Chip, the cats I saw on my street, seemed to be converging* on a central point: BLOSSOM LANE.

BLOSSOM LANE

*CONVERGING: When lots of things are headed for the same place where they will meet and, in this case, probably cause kitty chaos.

We already know that for some reason the cats of Puddleford are going crazy. Could this have something to do with Blossom Lane? Is that where the catnapper lives and has been luring the cats to night after night? Or is something else totally weird happening there?

We were there just this evening—it's where I met Poppy and Violet and their teams. It's a totally normal-looking cul-de-sac.

But thinking about it, Horatio did see a cat near his house. It's at times like this I really wish I had a working phone line in HQ.

Horatio was at home working on his toothpaste this evening, so he might have seen something. The cats would have been hard to miss with all the noise they were making. We'll pay him a visit when we do an emergency Mystery Girl search of the area first thing tomorrow morning.

Poppy will want to get to the festival with our inventions, but I'm sure she'll change her mind when she hears about this!

**Saturday
April 25th**

BLOSSOM
Lane

most mysterious
place in Puddleford?

Horatio's house

## 10:30 AM
## END OF BLOSSOM LANE, OUTSIDE
## HORATIO'S HOUSE

When Poppy and Violet arrived at my house this morning they couldn't believe what I'd discovered about the cats' movements. We came to Blossom Lane as quickly as we could.

"I thought it might look different somehow— you know, like maybe there would be screaming people being terrorized by demented cats," said Poppy, as we stared down the very neat, cherry tree-lined street.

neat street

"I don't understand how all the cats could be here without anyone noticing. Surely somebody would have reported something weird if this is the center of the Kitty Calamity," Violet said.

I was as shocked as Violet when I realized Blossom Lane was where the cats were headed. As well as last night, we walked down here on Wednesday and even looked in that big dumpster. Everything had seemed totally normal.

"This may look like one of the nicest streets in Puddleford, but that doesn't mean weird stuff isn't happening," I said. "Come on, let's ask if we can look in backyards."

"If anyone answers the door looking nervous, that might be the catnapper!" said Poppy.

SUSPICIOUS
LETTERS

Good point, Poppy. But as soon as we started knocking we encountered a fairly major problem. It seemed we were the only people who hadn't already headed to Puddleford Festival. By the time we reached Horatio's house at the very end of the street, we'd knocked on every single door with no answer, and of course Horatio wasn't there either.

"You don't think the cats have, you know, gone so crazy they've eaten everyone, do you?" Violet said.

ARGH!

hel!?!

"Don't be silly, Violet," Poppy said. "They'll be at the festival. You remember what the lines were like last year, don't you? If it hadn't been for this, I'd have said we should have left hours ago."

I knew Violet was being
silly, but part of me knew
what she meant. The
street is too quiet. As if
something weird might
be waiting behind one
of the flowery curtains
or lurking by the garden
gnomes.

"Maybe we should just head to the festival like
everyone else," Poppy said. "It's a shame not to
enter our inventions when we've got them with us.
The Fragrant Fishy dried out really well overnight."

Honestly, what sort of detective would rather
enter a competition when she could be getting
to the bottom of a missing cats case once and
for all?

"Poppy, we're not leaving without answers,"
I said.

We can't see into any of the backyards from the fronts of the houses, not without climbing over the tall gates that everyone has next to their garages. Maybe we could stand on a garbage can and jump over?

garbage can

HANG ON!

There! Under that bush! In Horatio's front yard! Something moved!

# THE CLAMBER* AGAINST CALAMITY

*CLAMBER: A frantic rush or scrabble to do something. Like solve the Kitty Calamity!

This is an accurate account of what happened next. Things got so totally crazy, there wasn't time to write it all down at the time.

WARNING: The next section contains details of Crazy Cat behavior that some individuals may find disturbing or distressing.

mystery girl clamber

## 10:40 AM
## HORATIO TWEED'S FRONT YARD

At first I wasn't sure if I was seeing things, but Violet
spotted it too and let out a startled squeak.
A matted, brown slimy blob-thing covered in twigs
and leaves staggered out from underneath a bush
next to the garage at the far side of Horatio's front
yard. I gasped as, with one wild eye, it scanned the
garden before fixing its eyes on us.

"CATNAPPING ALIEN!" Violet shrieked. "RUN!"

Poppy screamed and pulled my arm. But the Young Super Sleuth's Handbook says that a good detective is able to fight the urge to run in scary situations. After a closer look, I knew what we were dealing with.

mud

"Wait! It's a cat! It's covered in mud! I think it's . . . Henry!" I said.

Henry really did look weird. He was coated in a thick layer of gloopy mud, which covered one of his eyes, and there were moldy leaves stuck all over him. I could just make out part of his glittery collar and a few tufts of orange fur.

"Eurgh, I think you're right," Poppy said. "Has he been living in a garbage can or something?"

I wasn't sure, but after the disaster of last night's search, I was determined not to let Henry out of my sight. Wherever he was going next, I was going with him.

Carefully, I opened
Horatio's front gate
and took a few steps
across the front lawn.

Henry's tail twitched.

"Mariella! Be careful!" breathed Violet. "He looks
really on edge. I'd better put on the Calm-Cat Mitts."

I took another step forward. Henry hissed, turned,
and sprang over the six-foot-high gate at the side of
Henry's garage.

"Target is on the move. Follow that cat!" I called to
Poppy and Violet.

## 10:50 AM
## APPROACHING HORATIO'S BACKYARD

# Creeeeeak!

Luckily, Horatio's back gate wasn't locked.
Poppy, Violet, and I raced through it and burst out
onto Horatio's patio.

There was no sign of Henry. All we could see was
an old garden shed and large neatly mowed lawn
surrounded by a high, manicured
hedge. I felt like screaming—
it was so frustrating. The
cats were too quick
for us.

Everything looked totally normal. I could hear birds tweeting and bees buzzing, and actually, now that we were standing still . . .

Buurrrrrr. Buurrrrrrr.

"He can't have just vanished!" Poppy said.

"Sssh," I said. "Can you hear that?"

Buurrrrrrr. Buurrrrrrrr. Buurrrrrrrr.

"It's probably Horatio's washing machine on a spin cycle. Come on, let's go," Violet said.

That rumbling didn't sound like a washing machine to me.

"Violet! There's no way we are leaving," I said. "Search the garden!"

Poppy peered through Horatio's kitchen window. Violet set off nervously toward a stack of plant pots. I walked across the lawn toward the shed. The noise was louder here.

# Burrrrrr. Burrrrrrr. Burrrrrrr.

What was it? I looked through the shed window,
but all I could see were a few old plant pots and
pieces of broken inventions. It was only when I
walked around the side of the shed that I saw a
neat archway cut into the corner of the hedge.
There was another part to Horatio's garden!

# Burrrrr. Burrrrrr. Burr.

"The noise," I said, waving at Violet and Poppy
to follow. "It's coming from behind that hedge!"

Part of me didn't want to look—what if we'd
been right about catnapping aliens? Or werecats?
Or any of that unbelievable stuff?

My whole body was tense as we peered
around the leafy archway in the hedge.
What I saw took my breath away.

## 10:55 AM
## HORATIO'S VEGETABLE PATCH

Cats everywhere! The area,
which looked as if it had
once been used as a large
vegetable patch, was filled
with cats. Some were
stretched out in the sunshine,

others curled up snoozing, and others
rolled contentedly on their backs in
a mushy mess of mud. It looked like a
crazy, cat-infested swamp.

The noise was overwhelming. It was a deep rumble being made by the cats purring in delight at the same time.

# BURRR! PURRRRRR! PURRRRRR!

I looked around for Watson, but it was hard to pick out the identities of most of the cats. Poppy looked stunned. Violet wasn't scared anymore—she was really angry.

"HORATIO! What has he done to them? He's a deranged catnapper!" she spluttered, pointing at a cat, who was barely recognizable, as Joel Stetson in Year Four's tabby cat, Gingernut.

Gingernut had just wriggled away from a large huddle of cats who were rolling around on a particularly soggy mud patch. As well as mud, he was covered in patches of dripping blue gloop and, disturbingly, he was foaming at the mouth.

"Keep back! We don't know if it's safe to touch them! All this time Horatio was pretending to help us, but it was just to hide whatever crazy stuff he's been doing to these cats!" Violet shouted.

I stared at Gingernut, trying to make sense of it. I was sure that Violet must be wrong.

"Why would an inventor obsessed with experimental toothpaste want to hide hundreds of missing cats in his back yar—"

I didn't finish my sentence, though, because I was having an extreme detective deduction, brain-exploding moment.

". . . TOOTHPASTE! Gingernut is covered in toothpaste! That's what's foaming around his mouth!" I said. "Look—he loves it."

toothpaste! →

"Wait. Are you saying Horatio has been testing his toothpaste on innocent cats?" Violet said, horrified.

But that didn't make sense either. There are far easier ways to test toothpaste than on cats, and it definitely didn't explain why the cats had been escaping from their homes and running around Puddleford all week.

I looked closer at the group of cats nearby. Two of them slid sideways (Slinky and Binky, I think), revealing a rusted broken pipe jutting out of the ground. Toothpaste and foam oozed from it— ah-ha!

"Look!" I said. "Horatio isn't giving it to the cats—it's been leaking out of the drains! Judging by all the mud I'd say the whole area must have been flooded; before the cats ate it all, that is."

toothpaste

I couldn't help laughing. After spending the week imagining terrible things happening to Puddleford's cats, I was relieved they had just been here eating toothpaste the whole time.

I managed to compose myself enough to continue. "If Horatio poured his reject formulations down the sink the foaming could have burst the pipes!"

"So, this whole mystery has been caused by toothpaste?" Poppy said.

I couldn't believe it either.

"The smell must have been what was attracting them here!" I said. "Horatio told us he's been experimenting every night this week, so there would have been lots of toothpaste to eat."

It felt totally amazing to finally know what had happened, but I couldn't properly celebrate until I had Watson safely back home.

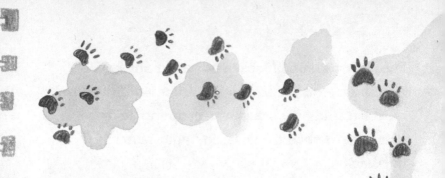

**11:10 AM**
**STILL IN HORATIO'S VEGETABLE PATCH**

Suddenly—

# MEEAAAAARRRGEEEOOWW!

One of the cats (I think it was Minky) lifted its head
and was sniffing the air. I took a few steps back in
shock. Minky wasn't the only one who seemed to
be coming out of her toothpaste trance. Soon, all the
cats were joining in with the crazy yowling.

# MEEAAARRGEEEOWW!
# MEOWarggh!

Poppy, Violet, and I looked at one another.
A moment ago we had neatly wrapped up the
mystery, and now chaos was erupting again.
I hadn't even had a chance to begin searching
for Watson.

"I told you we should be worried about werecats!"
Violet said, grabbing my arm.

The cats were up and darting past our feet.
Splattering minty-smelling mud all over us,
they ran off through the arch in the hedge.

## MEOWarggh!

The cats were escaping too quickly for my brain
to keep up—why were they going crazy again?
Was anyone even going to believe we'd solved
the case when soon, we'd have no missing cats,
a patch of mud and hardly any toothpaste . . .

Ah-ha! *Hardly any toothpaste.* I love it when
detective genius strikes.

"This has nothing to do with werecats!" I said. "Look, there's only a little bit of foam left here. They must be able to smell more toothpaste somewhere else!"

"Oh no, Mariella. Horatio's live experiment," Poppy said. "What if he's started it? I think the cats can smell his final toothpaste formulation! That's where they are heading!"

## MEOwargh! MEEEooooawoo!

Violet gasped. She must have been picturing the same scene I was—Horatio proudly demonstrating his new toothpaste in front of the whole of Puddleford, TV cameras rolling, with no idea that what he's actually invented is the world's most powerful, crazy cat paste.

ARGH!—

## SOLVING A MYSTERY TOO LATE

While every effort must be made to solve a mystery before a suspect evades capture or something terrible happens, there are occasions where you may solve a mystery too late. If this happens, take appropriate steps to insure your client isn't too disappointed.

## Use Positive Language:

At least you know who was behind this whole thing, even if we've got no chance of capturing them now.

I'll solve another mystery for you free of charge. Please do recommend me to your friends.

Have you thought of taking up a new hobby to distract yourself from the disappointment of the suspect getting away? Like knitting?

Tiddles was a great hamster, but there are lots of other great hamsters you can buy.

## These are Poor Excuses. Do Not Use Them:

That painting may have been priceless, but it was ugly. I did you a favor. You can get a nice new one now.

What did you expect? I'm a Young Super Sleuth, not an actual detective.

It's not my fault this happened. It was my brother/sister/uncle/dog/goldfish, etc. (Blame won't achieve anything.)

Your mystery was so boring I couldn't stay focused for long enough to solve it in time.

# TOP TIP

If you are receiving a high volume of angry phone calls, why not record an answering machine message apologizing and stating how unfortunate the whole thing is? That way you can continue on with solving your next mystery, before it's too late.

SORRY!

## 11:20 AM
## APPROACHING PUDDLEFORD FESTIVAL
## SHOWGROUND, PUDDLEFORD PARK

As Mystery Girls, we have extensive knowledge
of Puddleford and its secret shortcuts (essential for
surveillance situations), but I still wasn't sure we
had any chance of outrunning the cats.

Usually the high-speed chase part of solving
a mystery can be totally thrilling, but this was
different. Even though Horatio was behind the
whole Kitty Calamity, it was a total accident.
He'd been helping us with our inventions all
week because he really wanted us to solve
this case. We couldn't let the cats completely
ruin his dream of becoming a famous toothpaste
inventor.

"We'll never make it!" Poppy panted as we rushed along the footpath leading to the Puddleford Festival showground.

Cats called from behind us. They were close. Very close.

# MEEAAAAARRRGEEEOOWW!

Just ahead, at the end of the footpath, I could see the flashing lights of the fairground rides and the fluttering flags topping the different Best in Show marquees—and the line. It was huge!

"Mystery Girls coming through!" I screamed, as we barged past everyone. If we could get to Horatio before the cats did, we would be able to warn him.

"You can't do that!" somebody called.

The line

"Sorry! Cat disaster about to happen!" Violet called, sprinting past the shocked-looking ticket collector and under the huge sign over the entrance that read:

Welcome to the

PUDDLEFORD SHOW!

SPONSORED BY

kitty yum luxury cat products

WE LOVE YOUR CAT AS MUCH AS YOU DO!

Something told me that the people at Kitty Yum were definitely not going to love the toothpaste-crazed cats and they were going to regret having anything to do with Puddleford and this festival.

PUDDLEFORD SHOW · ADMIT ONE

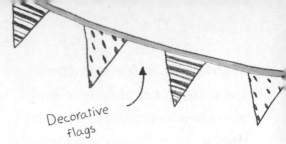

Decorative
flags

## 11:30 AM
## INSIDE PUDDLEFORD FESTIVAL
## SHOWGROUND

I scanned the crowds and marquees. There were
families eating hot dogs, a lady with a Labrador
dressed in a cowboy costume, decorative flags
fluttering in the breeze, Mom's Knit Your Own
Miniature Puddleford stand and cotton candy
sellers—but where was Horatio?

# MEEEoooooooooawooh!

yarn

The
festival

My heart raced. Violet gasped.
The cats were already here and
they knew exactly where to find
Horatio. Ahead, I could see Henry.
Four, five, six other cats flew past
our ankles, dodging through the
crowds and knocking people off balance.

"We might still be able to do something!"
I said. "Follow those cats!"

Mystery Girls do not abandon inventors
in need and they don't let a mystery they
have worked hard to solve come to an
embarrassing and messy conclusion!

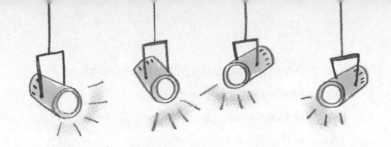

## 11:30 AM
## PIONEERS OF PUDDLEFORD DEMONSTRATION STAGE

We skidded around the corner of the Best Hat in Show marquee to catch a glimpse of a tail vanish into the large crowd that had gathered in front of a small stage. There on the stage stood a smiling Horatio.

The *Puddleford in Focus* TV crew were there filming. Dressed in his lab coat and safety goggles, Horatio looked totally professional, and totally unaware of what was about to happen.

With so many people watching, there was no way to get close enough to tell Horatio to stop. For the first time ever, the Mystery Girls were too late to save the day. All we could do was watch the disaster unfold.

Horatio was adding ingredients to a complicated system of tubes, beakers, flasks, and Bunsen burners. There was far more brewing equipment than Horatio had used in our assembly. And FAR more toothpaste.

"Mega Watt Grin Toothpaste! It promises an end to painful dentist trips and an end to fillings. Forever!" Horatio was beaming, as a stream of toothpaste squirted into a huge glass flask.

"There is enough here for everyone to take home a free sample," he added.

Oooooooh! The audience gasped in delight.

Violet looked at me, horrified. Nobody was
going to want the toothpaste when
they found out it was actually
mad-cat paste. Not that there
was likely to be any
toothpaste left if the cats
got to it first.

Poppy grabbed my arm. She'd spotted cats
prowling their way between the legs of the
audience. I spotted a matted but familiar fluffy
black and white tail and gasped. Watson. My own
trusty sidekick was about to play a part in ending
Horatio's career!

Looking up, I saw Henry appear on the canopy
above the stage. His eyes were fixed on the
now overflowing flask of toothpaste that
Horatio was holding up.

"I can't watch!" Violet said.

Henry dropped from the canopy onto the stage, landing lightly on his feet. His tail twitched, his eyes were firmly on Horatio—and the toothpaste.

Whispers rippled around the audience. Horatio stared at Henry in confusion. The toothpaste and mud from the garden had dried in patches now, making Henry's fur stick up all over the place.

# MEAAARRGEEOWW!

Horatio staggered backward. Cats were darting into the crowd from all sides, wailing and screeching. The crowd was looking around nervously.

"HENRY!" screamed Josie, who was standing near the stage. "That's my missing cat!"

Horatio jumped onto a stool,
holding the flask above his head.
Now there were thirty or more cats
circling him. Soon every cat
in Puddleford would be
on the stage.

It was clear the cats
were prepared to
go to great lengths
to get their crazy
furry paws on the
toothpaste.

Desperate for ideas, I looked around. There were
more cats on the burger van roof behind us. They
were under the balloon seller's cart to the right of
the stage, and creeping toward us through the
open doors of the Best Cat in Show tent.

The very empty Best Cat
in Show tent . . .

Hang on—that was it!

empty

BEST CAT IN SHOW

11:35 AM
PIONEERS OF PUDDLEFORD STAGE,
DODGING CATS

"HORATIO!" I called. "THROW THE
TOOTHPASTE IN THAT TENT!"

Horatio gazed at me, baffled.

"IT'S THE TOOTHPASTE! YOUR TOOTHPASTE
HAS MADE ALL THE CATS GO CRAZY!" Poppy
screamed.

Horatio looked at the jar and then
back at the cats. Then he closed
his eyes and flung his
experimental toothpaste
over the heads of
the crowd.

# Clink!

The flask landed in the tent. The contents spilled everywhere—instantly foaming up into a massive puddle.

"Oh no!" cried Horatio. "I thought I'd solved the foaming thing!"

I couldn't believe he was worried about that, faced with the chaos that had broken out in the crowd. Shocked owners were frantically calling their pets' names as the cats darted through the crowd with one objective—to get to the spilled toothpaste.

This was good. As the last cat ran inside the tent, Poppy and Violet secured the doors.

As I pushed my way toward the stage, I heard a squeaky voice shriek from the back of the crowd.

"WATSON! My big sister saved Watson! I LOVE YOU, WATSON, I'M COMING FOR YOU!"

Arthur! He was sitting on Dad's shoulders waving madly. It was totally embarrassing, but actually it had a really positive effect on the crowd. The mood turned from stunned silence to a relieved murmur. I ran up the steps to the stage.

HORRIFIED!

"I'm so sorry . . . I didn't realize the toothpaste would make all your cats crazy." Horatio was red-faced and flustered. "I can't seem to get anything right. I think it's best if I give up inventing with immediate effect."

I felt so sorry for him. Despite all our efforts, his demonstration had been a total disaster.

"Actually, we don't want you to give up inventing," a voice called.

A smartly-dressed woman stepped onto the stage with the Puddleford festival officials. I recognized her from her photograph in the *Puddleford Gazette*. It was Lizbeth Felange, owner of Kitty Yum Luxury Cat Products.

Lizbeth Felange!

"Kitty Yum would be very interested in talking to you about your recent invention. We pioneer new cat food technology, and your formulation is one of the most brilliant things I've ever seen. If cats love it, I love it," Lizbeth said.

The crowd gasped. I did too.

"The strength of the formula might need a bit of adjusting, but I'm sure an inventor genius such as yourself will have no problems with that," Lizbeth continued.

Horatio blushed and grinned.

Delighted

"Well, great!" I said into the microphone at the front of the stage. "Now, if all cat owners would like to form an orderly line, the Mystery Girls will return your cats to you."

The crowd cheered and yelled. Veronica was jumping up and down, hugging Joel Stetson from Year Four. Mom was standing next to Dad and Arthur now, waving a half-finished knitted festival marquee from her demonstration. Josie and Mrs. Bushell were sobbing with happiness.

The Kitty Calamity was officially wrapped up. And the most unexpected part so far, even more surprising than the cats going crazy—Horatio's experimental toothpaste might actually become cat food!

It looks as if our mystery-solving skills are just purr-fect. Ha!

HOORAY!

# Monday
# April 27th

Watson — at home!

## 8:30 PM
## MYSTERY GIRLS HQ, BEANBAG AREA,
## CHILLING WITH TRUSTY SIDEKICK, WATSON

All I wanted to do was to take Watson home, but there was still lots to do.

The cats were dopey and full after eating the toothpaste inside the Best Cat in Show tent, so to make sure none of them wandered off again, Poppy used the Kitty Spinner and the Fragrant Fishy to keep them entertained. Violet and I helped the owners find their pets. (Violet's allergies were kept under control by the Calm-Cat Mitts.)

Poppy didn't mind that we never entered our inventions into the Best in Show competition, not when they were being put to such good use. I was worried Miss Crumble might be annoyed, but she said she was totally proud and agreed that what we did was truly in the spirit of being a Pioneer of Puddleford.

Veronica's mom told Detective Sparks and festival officials that the police wouldn't have been able to rescue a hot dog from a bun and she dreaded to think what might have happened if the Mystery Girls hadn't been there. Detective Sparks looked totally embarrassed and had to apologize for not taking the missing cat problem more seriously.

Finding out he had caused the Kitty Calamity and that he had landed a deal to be a world-famous cat food maker all in one day was a bit much for Horatio to take in.

stunned

He was so flustered that the
Puddleford Show organizers
had to enlist an emergency
judge for the Inventions
competition. The lady who
had judged the Biggest Vegetable
competition clearly knew nothing about inventing,
because she chose Arthur's late entry Meow-Meow-
Love-Face as the winner. (Obviously, he wouldn't
have stood a chance if we'd entered.)

Anyway, it doesn't matter who won because the
Mystery Girls solved the Kitty Calamity, and Lizbeth
from Kitty Yum noticed we are total geniuses too.
Before she whisked Horatio away in her pink limo,
she said she had been blown away when she saw
the Kitty Spinner in action. She's taken the Kitty
Spinner, the Fragrant Fishy, and the Calm-Cat Mitts
to show her team. Cool!

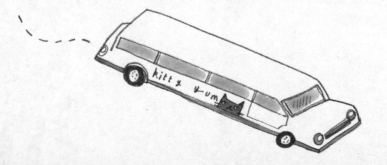

We heard from Horatio this morning and he said he'll be working non-stop at Kitty Yum headquarters until the recipe is perfect. It will still be irresistible to cats, but won't actually make them crazy like the toothpaste version did.

Horatio hasn't got long to figure that out, because Kitty Yum haven't wasted any time advertising the launch date for the new Kitty Yum-a-licious cat food. They say this new range is pioneering and will change cat food forever. It's going to be available in the shops in a few weeks!

kitty
Yum-a-licious

And that's not the last unbelievable news. Watson is playing a starring role in the TV advertisement, along with all the other Puddleford cats that went missing!

star!
cat

After school today, Kitty Yum arranged for Horatio to be filmed feeding the cats. The final advertisement is going to be great—Horatio looked totally professional wearing a Kitty Yum lab coat, while all the cats purred around him. Watson got paid in free test samples of Kitty-Yum-a-licious.

We have to fill in a form and say which flavor Watson preferred, but it's hard to tell because he just swallows them all in five seconds without even chewing.

(We had to give Watson a bath before filming, and under all the crusty mud was the fake mustache he was wearing when he went missing! It's all clean and just smells a little minty.)

minty
fresh!

cat wash

The cat owners were so happy to get their pets back that they haven't blamed Horatio for all the trouble. On the *Puddleford in Focus* TV special on Sunday night, he came across really well, like a misunderstood science genius. They said he was a true Pioneer of Puddleford and was bound to take the cat food world by storm.

After all that, I only had time to write up our case report. Read on to find out how the Mystery Girls solved one of the most baffling and mysterious cases ever.

# KITTY CALAMITY CASE REPORT

Horatio's house

The Kitty Calamity was unintentionally caused by local inventor, Horatio Tweed. Unbeknownst to Horatio, the experimental toothpaste he had been brewing late at night attracted cats from the surrounding area. They found the smell irresistible.

We now know that the rare Amazonian Pooka-Pooka* leaf used as a cleaning agent in Horatio's toothpaste drove the cats wild in the same way catnip does—only about a million times stronger. Like catnip, the smell is undetectable by humans.

Pooka-Pooka leaf

Horatio didn't notice the cats because he was deep in concentration. And also since Horatio listens to loud music during experiments, because it helps him to think of great ideas.

The only neighbor whose house overlooks Horatio's backyard is Mrs. Morris, aged eighty-six. She wasn't able to see the vegetable patch covered in cats because she is extremely near-sighted. The tall hedge also acted as a soundproofing wall so that the rumbling noise made by all the cats purring at once couldn't be heard outside Horatio's backyard.

mrs. Morris

We think the crazy cat yowling wasn't so bad in the immediate area of Blossom Lane because the cats were happily eating the toothpaste rather than desperately trying to find it. That's why none of Horatio's other neighbors noticed anything odd.

Horatio worked late into the night, so that's why so many cats disappeared in the middle of the night and why sleeping residents didn't see them racing down Blossom Lane.

The high doses of the Pooka-Pooka leaf had a powerful effect on the cats. Some were so full they passed out all day under bushes in Horatio's backyard, but others were spotted acting completely out of character, ignoring their owners and refusing to return home.

The breakthrough that solved the case came after a search party led by the Mystery Girls. Cats were spotted darting across rooftops and leaping over fences. Expert Mystery Girl analysis of these cat-like movements showed that all cats were headed for a central point—Blossom Lane.

An emergency search revealed the missing cats still eating their way through the multiple batches of foamed-up toothpaste Horatio had made while trying to perfect his toothpaste recipe the previous evening.

We are pleased to report that after a few days away from the experimental toothpaste, the cats have returned to their normal selves. (Although a little bit chubbier than before.)

## CASE CLOSED

**NOTE:** Kitty Yum have assured cat owners that the new formulation cat food won't make the cats go crazy. It is hoped that the food will be so delicious that cats will be far less likely to ever wander off and go missing again. (Hooray!)

**\*POOKA-POOKA LEAF:** What Horatio didn't know was that the Rara tribe living in the remote area where the leaf grows used it as a highly effective tooth polisher and also to tame wild jaguars so they could be kept as pets. The doses given to the domestic cats of Puddleford were around one hundred times higher than those given to jaguars, resulting in the manic cat behavior.

tame

The mystery Girls